Adele and Tom
The Portrait of a Marriage

By
Chella Courington

Published By

Breaking Rules Publishing

Soft Cover – 10344
Published by Breaking Rules Publishing
Pompano Beach, Florida
www.breakingrulespublishing.com

ACKNOWLEDGMENTS

I thank my mentor and friend, Robin Lippincott, for his guidance and advice.

I thank my loving and literary husband, Ted Chiles, always my first and last reader.

Excerpts from the novella appear in the following anthologies and journals: *Cacti Fur, Doorknobs and BodyPaint, Every Day Fiction, Eyedrum Periodically, Fiddleblack, Florida Flash: A Prompt-Based Christmas Anthology, riverbabble, Southeast Fiction, Sparks of Consciousness, Up, Do Flash Fiction by Women Writers, Ponder Savant, borrowed solace,* and *Spelk.*

Dedicated to my husband Ted, who's a lot nicer than Tom.

Chapter 1

Adele knew she was in trouble when Tom's long strides carried him in on that September night at Kat and Harry's Café. White button-down shirt and jeans, black hair brushing his collar. He did not sense trouble when he sat at the bar, one stool between them, ordered a stout and placed his cigarettes near the ashtray. She had arrived in Montgomery, Alabama, in 1988, and he in 1990. Each armored in a Ph.D., hers in Literature and his in Economics. Each with a divorce, motivating a change, a shift to someplace else.

Then the awkward moment. The time silence hung in the air, neither he nor she looked up, heads down studying their drinks, staring at anything to keep from saying the first word, being the one ever responsible. Adele, more than Tom, was used to being hit on, silly lines that men still boys toss, most times nothing, but then the occasional bite from the woman who's been sitting too long alone and conversation happens. Lips play over the second and third beers until they wind up in the back booth, darker than the bar, thighs touching, talking of Buffalo Springfield and William Burroughs to pizza for breakfast and hangovers that last until the next night.

Chapter 2

At a summer solstice party in Santa Barbara, California, fifteen years later, Mary with a flute of sparkling wine toasted Tom and Adele as the perfect couple. They turned to each other and kissed though she felt oddly out of time as if the toast were premature. If perfect meant having all the desirable elements, she produced a smile that hid the reverse—the cracks and empty places. She listened to him speak as he told of days together writing at home and breaking for an Americano.

"Tell Mary about your new story," she said.

"Negative Space," Tom said. "Adele made it work, varying syntax, moving subjects to the end and staying with the image until it cracked open, releasing *je ne sais quoi.*"

She loved his expression of gratitude, that he saw her as a participant in his writing life. But she felt different, too much of a feminist to think of herself as a helper. She was a writer who sensed her confidence receding, being pulled under by his success. His hand, the one without a flute, touched her shoulder.

Chapter 3

When they first dated, she always ordered fish, any fish on the menu—mackerel, halibut, sea bass, cod; she didn't choose fish because she thought it tasted good; in fact, she abhorred the smell, fishy like the boats at Oyster Bay, but she thought it good for her, high in protein, vitamin B and D, and omega 3 fatty acids; yet even more, she liked the way she looked eating fish and wanted others to see her taking small bites of white, flaky flesh, lifting the delicacy with grace to her lips then laying it on her tongue to begin the process of mastication, a word her mother used often because her mother thought often about the body and what she learned from biology, and no one of her mother's era, particularly her mother's friends, would use a common word like chew, something cows did to cud not civilized human beings to flaky white fish.

Chapter 4

Some nights Adele was lulled to sleep by the television, drifting into peace, Gray purring, touching her with his paw. Other nights, Tom woke Adele to remove her glasses before turning off the lights. She lay there, mulling over what she avoided in light. A daughter never far, who would be in her twenties if Adele and Tom had pursued her, if Adele had taken the fertility drugs, brushed away her fear of being ambushed by her body. But Tom and Dr. Gibbs encouraged her to forget about having a child.

"You can take the meds and still never get pregnant. Here are the statistics," said the doctor, handing her a page of numbers. An alien language, lifeless and sterile.

"Maybe we can adopt," she said.

Tom was silent. After a pause hoarding oxygen, he asked, "But Adele, don't you want a baby who has us running through her?"

To have or not to have was her struggle that Tom won. Would it be different if Tom and Dr. Gibbs

were women? Would she have a daughter today, someone who called every night and asked how long it took to roast a chicken or if graduate school was worth the long nights and neglected friends? But why did Adele do this to herself, swim in the past, speculating over choices that now seemed irrelevant because behind? Why was she constantly pulled back? She remembered an essay by Annie Dillard about weasels, those cute mustelids maligned by popular culture. Dillard said we can learn something from the instinctual life. Unburdened by memory and hope. Alive in the moment, aware of what we see now and nothing more. Maybe we can learn balance, Adele thought, her memories hushed by sleep

Chapter 5

Tom would like that, Adele thought, a pound of French Roast from the French Press on State Street, a new coffeehouse in an old storefront, each cup pressed to perfection. Coarse grounds trapped beneath wire, caged at the beaker's bottom for four minutes, not longer, not hours like the boy in the black and white Boris Karloff movie who screams until a murder of crows lifts the cage and drops it softly in the Adirondacks. Thereafter, Adele flinched at the sight of wire any wire: True Hardware, a nightmare; her father's garage, an inquisition; construction sites, an ordeal. But a French press was different, wire too small to hurt for long.

"Would you like a croissant?" the barista asked.

"Not today," she said.

Tom would eat one without a qualm, without worry if he weighed less yesterday than tomorrow. But she bounced from scale to scale, watching the needle turn, feeling her skin stretch with each taste, each teasing of her tongue. How she hated the morning after.

"No éclair? No Palmier?"

Couldn't the young barista with his ponytail see her agony, smell her fear, how he was tempting her, how easily she gave in to what was offered, only to regret.

Chapter 6

Tom stopped under a magnolia tree, breathing harder than usual. Maybe the heat or humidity or his third drink at lunch.

"Where was our first Cajun martini?" he asked.

"Le Petit Theatre," Adele said, tracing the bow of her lip like a girl-in-waiting for her first kiss.

"When Alec Baldwin played Stanley?"

"Yes, in the courtyard during intermission. I wore black velvet pants and you a silk jacket."

Adele and Tom were younger then and believed life imitated art, quaffing vodka under screams and splitting muffulettas in Jackson's shadow.

"Did we sober up?" she asked.

"At the Café du Monde," he said, remembering how the velvet clung to her ass.

After Cajun martinis they ate gumbo and drank hurricanes down Bourbon to Toulouse and eventually the river. He bummed a cigarette from a trumpet player, floating a dollar into his case. She chastised him even as she stole a drag. Later, as always, as they must, they ate beignets and sipped café au lait. In a silver suit and tie the silver mime stood among back and forth travelers who bought jewelry and coins and Tarot readings from vendors on the square. The shiny wizard arrested time on a point of no circumference while women turned girls and retreated. Somewhere close, their beaux advanced without consent when Adele and Tom passed through the *Pontalba porte cochere,* already taken.

Chapter 7

Tom stroked Adele's cheek, soft as when they married and would lie, touching, for hours on the patch quilt his mom made for his graduation. Adele had taught him affection, sliding her fingers down his arm, slowly, stopping as they talked of how they wanted their lives to unfold. Then they moved together and separately, sharing movies and pizza and long afternoons on the Gulf, still building castles with moats and lookouts, swept away by the tide, only the toothpick flags surviving. They liked being kids again but play dates became fewer and fewer.

Chapter 8

She was sad. She was sick. Fighting a nasty cold, sneezing into her sleeve when she couldn't reach a tissue, her sinuses stuffed and achy. And, of course, she received a rejection on her most recent submission with the usual response: *We received many well written, compelling stories but, unfortunately, we will not be able to use yours. We wish you the best of luck placing it elsewhere.* She deleted it, wiped into oblivion, called the editor a sexist worm, wanted to hit reply with fuck you. Another minus sign for what she wanted to create. Reaching for a sugar-free cough drop, she slipped under the covers and called Gray who stayed at her feet, tail swishing, eyes closed, ignoring her.

Chapter 9

"What do you think of my story?" Tom asked, sitting on the couch perpendicular to her.

"I like it. Your character reminds me of Abner Snopes," Adele said and handed him his manuscript.

"Snopes, the barnburner and horse thief? Are you kidding?"

"No. Your art collector has Snopes' need to control."

He stared at the draft, pen marks turning the pages into illuminated squiggles. She wrapped her fingers around the white mug. Should she zap it? Warm coffee took her home. He had asked her to edit in red but then slumped against the cushions.

"The collector's not a scoundrel whose son abandons him," Tom said.

"Sure, Snopes is openly dishonest. But so is your collector who buys cheap from street artists who paint flamingoes and funky chickens on plywood," Adele said. "The collector knows Outsider Art can claim big bucks in the right galleries," her hand still holding her cup, her voice rising a couple of notes. She couldn't argue with him. He was still an economist, logical from point A through the alphabet, condensing life to an equation.

"Arbitrage is the moral equivalent of arson?" he asked. "Aren't you forgetting there are laws against stealing and destroying property?"

"I didn't say that."

She answered so quietly that he leaned closer, asked her to repeat herself, took her free hand.

"All the collector has is passion, the same with Snopes. Men of fire without an art form," she said and released his hand.

Chapter 10

Adele knew she could write, she'd always written and written well by the moderate standards of the schools in her small town. In the eighth grade she wrote her first poem for Mrs. Smothers about a white cat trapped in the neighbor's basement, but Mrs. Smothers did not choose to read her poem in class, reading Pam Walker's about thunder and lightning and a lost girl. Adele felt rejected but kept writing and her next poem was about thunder and lightning and a lost boy. Mrs. Smothers liked lost children and read that poem aloud. Adele felt ecstatic.

Traveling in and out with words, she had stacks of diaries in pastel shades, pink and lime being her favorite, always with lock and key, from the fifth grade on. It all started under the sheets with Nancy Drew and a flashlight. Her idol had a roadster and solved mysteries. Adele was too young to drive but started keeping secrets. She played with words more than her next-door neighbor, letters exploding and collapsing, taking her places.

Words were marvelous; a word her mother used when life was full of wonder and Henny Penny didn't think the sky was falling. Those moments were exquisite, according to her mother and her mother's mother, and she wanted to store them in her diary. Today I saw a hummingbird around the red tube flowers. Dad took me to the Ringling Brothers Circus today and we ate the largest cotton candy ever made. Mom and I saw *Gone with the Wind* on TV today. Dad is handsome like Rhett Butler. She was at home in her diaries but began calling them journals in college.

Years later Tom appeared. She loved him. He became a writer too but long after Adele. He never kept a journal and started writing when she told him it's a good way to work out problems. But now the problem was the writing. She began to feel uncomfortable in her own words, doing the thing she loved, seeing syllables stretch into words, words into poems, and poems into short prose. What she once thought natural, thinking out loud on paper or now most of the time on screen, seemed awkward, or she thought so. She felt lost somewhere between her words and his. How he urged her to go into scene and opened her manuscript where she and he, or two people like them, discussed what a reader wanted. She, not the character, turned to him, "I need to go to the toilet. Can we talk about this later?"

And hiding in the bathroom, Adele knew what she was doing, no longer able to bear his instruction. He easily put his characters into tension, lots of dialogue with even the right amount of description. And he wanted to shake her characters out of their solipsism, move them out of their heads into a conversation with each other. But she was not like that, she was not a conversational creature and rarely thought that kind of existence would appeal to her characters. They looked inward like the eyes of Milton after his glaucoma; they explored the abyss of their own interior with wretched delight, always wanting to go to the darkest place within, the shadiest part of their being.

But how could she tell him that, how could she say it was futile having her characters speak, they were beings locked inside her journals and refused to be pushed into a public spectacle. But she knew he would win. Thunder and lightning for the reader. He would be the one to receive awards while she raveled the thoughts and emotions of her character night after night, refusing that a finer existence could be found.

Chapter 11

In a green tunic the barefoot man held the smoke in his hands and rubbed it over their shoes and jeans, chests and faces.

"Sage will protect you," the man muttered and turned to the next couple.

"What now?" Tom asked.

"We wait for the guide," Adele said.

This was how they got to the Funk Zone, Santa Barbara's Left Bank.

"To broaden our awareness of how we fill physical space," she said.

He, who had apologized for their last movie choice three times, deferred.

"I already know. You're 5'9", weigh 159; I'm 5'11," weighed 200," he said

She didn't smile.

Through a yin yang beaded curtain, the guide led them up a narrow staircase to a black room, two women in tights suspended on aerial cables. No music, no voice, a white light on black encased muscle and bone twisting around thick wire, arms pulling the other closer until torsos and heads melded, energy flowing through them like a circuit with no breaker. Adele's right hand touched Tom's, vessels raised and soft. With the tip of her forefinger, she traced the longest from his wrist over bone through knuckles to the base of his middle finger. She remembered the sudden horrification traveling up her arms in freshman biology when the instructor lifted his hand and said: "Look at your fingertips. They are more sensitive than your penis or clitoris." She'd felt warm and wet, sucking on her middle finger to test the correlation and understood that perhaps masturbation would be the ultimate sexual sensation and that her fingers must be kept clean and moisturized for moments like this when standing together in public, witnessing the foreplay of two bodies on wire, their heat rising, filling the room with musk and yearning so that now Adele turned to Tom, her fingertips teaching his veins to follow her out of the room, down the narrow stairs, and past the barefoot man in green to a dark place under the night.

Chapter 12

He did not want depression. She preferred sourdough toast and fig preserves. He preferred chocolate croissants and hardly ever dreamed of the dead. She did.

Some nights her mother and father returned, not always together, not always to her. Two nights ago, a stranger walked into the kitchen, wearing her father's Irish cable cardigan. Where did you get that sweater? she asked. A gift from your father. He's back home, the stranger said. She walked into her parents' bedroom on Martling Road, not their last house but their first. She could hear the shower and her father talking to her mother. She stood there until the door opened. In his white terry cloth robe her father walked past. She called for her mother and woke up to Tom shaking her.

"You're crying," he said.

Chapter 13

.

After her anxiety attack, Dr. Kent ordered an echocardiogram. Wires stuck to her chest, the nurse pulled Adele's shoulders forward as she lay on her left side.

"Don't move until the red light blinks."

A screen reflected a half moon wobbling in and out of darkness, sloshing to every beat. White lines of lightning tore through, and the nurse froze the image, jotted on her clipboard.

"What are those?" Adele asked.

"I'm measuring the left ventricle," the nurse said.

Adele looked away at the stress-test walker and blood pressure cuff. Closed her eyes, the sloshing comforted her. She imagined walking into the Pacific, waves washing her, leaving traces of salt.

Six weeks ago in Portland, Oregon, their first vacation since her father died, Adele lay in the hotel bed, ice wrapped in a washcloth on her forehead.

"You're okay," Tom said and read from the Mayo Clinic Website on his iPad. "Hold ice on your brow and breathe deeply."

She tried to believe him. But she kept her left index finger on her sports watch, her pulse climbing, moving between 130 and 148.

"Stop counting. One long breath, hold, and breathe out," he said.

Twenty minutes later he fell asleep, his hand on her left thigh as she measured her pulse, 141 on the illuminated face. That night his snore soothed her and she snuggled against his back. Her father wanted to drift into a deep sleep and let the water take him away. She wanted sleep too, shutting out the ringing and throbbing.

"You can dress now and go back to the waiting room," said the nurse, shaking Adele's shoulder.

When she walked in, Tom's finger moved across the iPad and turned the imagined page.

Chapter 14

Adele sometimes felt as if she lived in another era, maybe George Eliot's Midlands or Fanny Burney's London, a time when novels provided models of behavior, particularly for those girls and women outside the circle of convention, waiting for moments when they could slip up to their room under the pretense of a headache and write in their journal while below the ladies drank tea and knitted, passing down wedding knots to their daughters. Yes, Adele always felt like an import, or a cracked china cup, the one with green trim and pink azaleas that belonged to Aunt May, pushed to the corner of the second shelf, seen only at Christmas or Thanksgiving when the meat plate also trimmed in green was gently lifted, washed again and placed in the center of the table, a place Aunt May or her teacup never occupied because she was a teacher who never married, spending weekends at her cabin in Boone, North Carolina, re-reading all of Eliot's novels from *Adam Bede* to *Daniel Deronda*.

Adele's mother dropped by once on a trip through the Smoky Mountains and said the house was small, a tan cottage and brown shutters, walls of bookcases, light oak with etched moldings, and Aunt May's housemate, a tall woman in khakis and a blue Oxford shirt, a woman none of the family had heard about. They drank tea and ate cucumber sandwiches, crust trimmed in the British fashion, while Aunt May and her housemate talked of plans to hike the Appalachian Trail, or as much as they could in July and August before school started. Adele's mother mentioned that day often, the only time she heard Aunt May giggle and saw her smile. Holding the cup in her left palm, Adele looked at the hairline fracture between the flowers and could hear a faint laugh.

Chapter 15

Tom was driving the Honda, not a convertible though he had wanted a rag top for sunny days, south to Malibu, and Adele was sitting next to the Pacific watching surfers through glass, afraid of car drafts paralyzing facial muscles, causing one side to droop and freeze the eye open.

"Poetry is a point and a point fixes the location of two values," Tom said.

"What?"

"X and Y are coordinates of the point."

"What?"

"Solving the function of our love."

"You're very disturbed" and Adele put her hand on his right thigh, nearer the top than the knee but not at the end point as he might say. She rarely understood concepts grounded in math and economics, simply trying to remember to say the word *economics* with the long e instead of the short.

"I'm merely looking at life through a different lens," Tom said.

She much preferred his photographic metaphor because, to be honest, Adele often thought of focus and light, having shot a Canon AF at WHNT when he was still trying to solve the intersection of supply & demand.

"So, what is Y?" she asked.

Chapter 16

Adele and Tom made it to Alabama, more specifically Sand Mountain, to visit her brother. Since her father died, Adele had been there once. It was too hard to drive into those dark hills of fast food and Piggly Wiggly without feeling her voice crack and sadness begin to well. When a kid, Adele dreamed of leaving the place, going to Atlanta or Gainesville, anywhere away from rednecks and racists. But she loved her mom and dad and home, her physical home inside a brick structure built in the 20s with a long hall, grid floor furnace in the middle, three bedrooms, kitchen, dining room and family room. Weekends were for holing up with Nancy Drew and watching the silhouetted ballerinas never pirouetting beyond their frame. Adele would dream of how one night they would kick the wood with their padded tough toes and arch their legs onto the greenish blue wall, clasping hands, rising on one toe, each lifting her other leg like the swan she so desired to become. Lovely feathered bird with a neck to grace the lake and wings to float barely above the water, gliding endlessly until Venus shone just above the horizon and they looked for a willow cover for the night.

Chapter 17

"My brother has aged since Christmas," Adele said to Tom as they were leaving her brother's investment office.

"He is walking like an old man, slumping forward," Tom said.

"Do you think he's in pain?" she asked, seeing him now barely thirteen, hoisting her five-year-old self on his shoulders when her feet got tired.

"I adored him," Adele said. "He and his first girlfriend took me to the drive-in."

"That's amazing," Tom said. "My sister and I rarely spoke till I was in my 20s."

"Watch out. The red truck with the deer lights may pull out."

Worse than Highway 1 in California, 431 lets you cross lanes almost anywhere. Individual rights in this state are sacrosanct if they involve cars, guns, and ethnicities. Recently some senator from Dekalb County decided to become the Enforcer of immigrant regulations and more than half the state's farm workers found new land, leaving the farmers and the legislators in a brouhaha not unlike the ructions Adele grew up with—unions trying to organize the local radio station, white parents accusing the black students of bullying their kids at school.

"Tom, I so wish I could have a real conversation with my brother. How can your life with somebody start in such deep affection and pool in ten-word conversations?"

"He is what he is, Adele. You love him and have to accept this. He's 60."

"I know, but I keep hoping this time will be different."

"And you wind up disappointed," Tom said, turning into the brother's gravel drive again at his home.

Chapter 18

At night Tom wrapped himself in the quilt, emitting snores not like her father's that rattled half the house but like a hand drill, heard through a wall. Sleep began for him at 11:30 p.m. while she lay in the dark listening to her body. Using the nightlight to read the counter on her running watch, she measured her pulse three times before putting away the light and the watch. Why three? It seemed like a number that never betrayed her. She had had three best friends from seventh through twelfth grades, her birthday was March 3, and when she was three, her mother drew the number in her right palm with a red magic marker, glowing under the sheets six straight nights. So she almost always did her routines in threes. Brushed her teeth three minutes, checked the lock three times before leaving, and always picked flowers in threes. Tom had been the third to ask.

Chapter 19

Mission bells reverberating vibrating swinging her back and forth in a rope hammock in April, gentle April, seconds, maybe minutes, each clang closer to waking her. Ten years and only now she heard the bells, glorious ringing, a Lenten holiday perhaps, if still in London a Whitsun wedding but that was summer, not spring. She woke lying next to Tom, his snores muffled by bells ringing from a 6 by 8 iPad draped in black, leaning like a headstone. She walked around the bed, lifted the cover, slid the touch to stop, and roused him.

Chapter 20

Adele had never read *You Can't Go Home Again* but Thomas Wolfe was a familiar name, being a Southern writer from North Carolina and dying young like many of the great Romantics. Wolfe was a legend her mother talked about, reading his novels then hiding them in brown paper sacks, afraid of her own desire to dig beneath the surface, behavior that polite young gentlemen and ladies were never to indulge though Adele felt her mother often peered over the edge. Trying to see what was forbidden and never speaking of what she saw.

Adele knew how close women came to being engulfed by men and their economic power. Adele's grandmother married a small-town merchant twenty years older, a dapper gent who held her on a tight rein as he did his horses. But she broke free, found fun and companionship in the young men who wandered up the mountain from Gadsden or passed through on their way to Birmingham. Finally, Adele's grandfather declared his red-headed wife unfit to raise their daughter, their only child, Adele's mother, and sent her to Miss Howard's School for Girls at the age of fourteen, leaving instructions that his daughter was to receive no mail until Miss Howard had read the letter to ensure it was not from a young man.

Adele's mother grew up longing for whatever lay hidden inside the envelope and behind the door, the daughter of a flapper who longed for life beyond restraint. But she, like her mother, finally was caught in a two-bedroom, one-bath house with a screaming child and a husband always asking for something more. Adele's mother turned to Wolfe and Carson McCullers. Twenty years after her mother had died, Adele hoped one way to her mother's heart was through the authors she had read under cover.

Chapter 21

Adele looked out at the two avocado trees, dark green bell-shaped fruit, clustered in twos and threes, sometimes fours, light filtered through the leaves, warming, waiting for the moment the weight would become unbearable, the limb begin to sag and later, maybe a week later, drop its legacy that Adele would pick up, skin yielding to her touch. She would place it on the bamboo block, her knife slicing from top to bottom, open the halves delicately and spear the stone, lifting it from oily yellow pulp, the very flesh she would rub with sea salt. Her first bite of the season.

Chapter 22

At the back table near the espresso machines, Tom sat writing when Adele walked in.

"Want to buy me a vanilla latte?" she asked.

Starbucks was his refuge away from home. Before he ordered, the barista would ask decaf Americano, two shots? He liked being known there, the feeling of welcome, of being valued. The hours lost in writing, a world compactly his own, white noise sealing tight, possible characters walking through the door, conversations to overhear.

"There's a Chihuahua-mix rescue puppy at the Montecito Pet Shop," she said.

Sometimes he would tell her he was working and didn't want to be interrupted. She had a way of forgetting boundaries when she wanted to talk.

"Is it yappy?" he asked.

"Not really. When I walked to the fence, he came running, big brown eyes, little paws stretching to reach me," she said. "There were two other people watching, but the puppy came to me as if he wanted to climb into my arms and go home. He's neutered and has had his shots."

"I'm allergic to dogs," he said.

"I'm allergic to cats," she said.

"Touché."

He heard her longing, her need to care for life beyond them. The time Gray was sick, she fed him with an eyedropper for three weeks. She and Gray were inseparable though Tom sometimes wished the cat didn't sleep on a pillow between them.

They sat sipping their coffees. A young girl with green hair looking all of eighteen came in carrying a Hello Kitty computer bag.

"What about Gray?" he asked. "He might move to the top of the bookcase."

"I called Dr. L who said cats aren't bothered so much by a different species. What I like about the pup is he's small and at max will weigh about ten pounds, Gray's weight."

Tom thought Adele looked teary. He knew why she was here. The girl with the green hair stood at the counter, coffee in hand, searching for a place to sit. He saved chapter twenty-three and closed his laptop, nodded and smiled to the girl.

Chapter 23

Adele sat at his table, writing in her moleskin journal, waiting for Tom. Together they would visit the Chihuahua-mix again, big brown eyes, so different from their Zen cat, window sleeping, fur rising and falling.

Her vanilla latte still warm, she noticed a woman, perhaps ten years older than she, and a girl, really a woman the age of her students, talking close, probably mother and daughter on a Saturday outing, the mother proud of her grown daughter but missing those times she followed the mother from room to room, asking to help, tugging at her dress.

Adele was writing about the June Saturday she and Tom drove to Gulf Shores on a lark, to drink Schlitz in the waves and listen to blues at the Flora-Bama. They slept on the beach, hidden behind dunes, and took sponge baths at the gas station.

Looking up, she saw the mother and daughter across from her laughing, a blueberry muffin broken and crumbled on a plate. The older woman brushed the girl's face, not with a mother's touch. Finger tips slid down the jawline, down the throat, across the collarbone and then stopped, stopped perhaps because the women were in public, at the edge of the T-shirt. The young woman, her eyes partly closed, leaned back against the padded bench.

Adele remembered her uncle with a much younger woman, the fountain of youth, someone who wasn't even born when he was a Captain in Vietnam. Adele thought May-December relationships were a male thing, power and patriarchy.

The older woman, her hair resembling the cut of an aging English rock star four albums from his last hit, scanned the tables, smiling. The girl emerged from her long, auburn curls. They stood, gathering their white and green paper cups, and walked out. A new moon in an old moon's arms.

Chapter 24

It was nighttime and Tom and Adele were in bed reading and eating vanilla ice cream, homemade from Tom's machine, all the machines belonged to Tom in Adele's mind. Ice cream was the only dessert Adele dreamed of besides cheesecake, graham cracker crust loaded with cream cheese and sour cream, browned around the edges, heavy and tall, good with coffee for breakfast. Last night Adele dreamed she was sitting on the towel that covered the newspaper that covered the ice her Dad's ice-cream canister was packed in. As he turned the handle, her butt got colder and colder.

"Dad, I'm freezing," she said.

"Just a few more minutes," he said.

Suddenly, she was perched on a block of ice alone in the snow, her lips nearly frozen shut, eyelids so heavy she squinted through a crack. Snow without houses or trees or any living thing as far as she could see when she heard a high-pitched trill and wings spread like a fan in front of her. Adele stood, slowly stretching her arms around his neck, feathers prickly with ice, and felt her feet lift with grace.

Chapter 25

Adele never thought of chores before noon, if then, for she eased into the day as she liked to say of the way she slipped out of bed, asking Tom for a cup of coffee before kissing him on the cheek. On her nightshirt, a woman with red pouty lips and a black boa announced, "I am the pink flamingo on the great lawn of life." Adele then opened her computer and dropped behind the screen while Tom put plates and cups in the dishwasher. She knew the Muslim Brotherhood was storming the streets in Cairo to protest Morsi's deposition and that President Assad denied the use of chemical weapons against his own people in Syria. But Adele deferred thought of the outside world until after she explored what lay between sleeping and waking, the fuzzy unconscious space close to her inner life, the place she could be eight again, her mother folding towels, aligning the corners, placing the rounded ends at the outside edge of the shelf so when you opened the door, you saw curves of terry cloth, not a ragged fringe with hanging threads.

Adele thought her mother an angel in the house, painting the walls a pale shade of blue to bring the sky and ocean inside, arranging sweet peas for almost every room, their wavy blossoms scenting the air. She knew how to use nails and a hammer, slinging a carpenter's belt around her waist to fix a flimsy leg on the kitchen table or a loose arm on the rocker. She took Adele on walks collecting red and orange leaves that Adele would trace on onionskin, cut, and color. She would carry the leaves and their replicas to her mother who would string them on rainbow yarn and drape across the mantel above the gas logs.

Chapter 26

When Adele left Alabama and moved West, she wrote about growing up in the Appalachians, mostly lined poetry ending with a slap across the face or sex in the backseat of a black Trans Am, barely more than the lyrics of a country song but stuff she had to get rid of, baggage she had to burn to clear the way for something new, starting with bits of life located no place specifically, rising in the moment when she brushed her shoulder against the door or detected a new wrinkle at the corner of her mouth and realized that her life was indeed unique, unfolding with each breath, a self emerging apart from the red clay of Sand Mountain, the dark soil of Santa Barbara.

Place was a point, arbitrary and outside her heart, her gut, and the real stuff of who she was, who she hoped to be, was just beginning to find shape and Adele believed in time, rocks uncovering as wear smoothed their edges, water back and forth until she could hold the stone in her palm, warm against her skin, and she felt steady in this new strength, writing about someone close to her, a teacher who spends her life working with words so when read aloud they give students goose bumps.

Chapter 27

Tom observed the line grow, caffeine before work. Balzac allegedly drank fifty cups a day and when that was not enough to fire his brain, began to eat coffee beans. Tom liked his coffee too, running up a $200 bill at Starbucks before buying a French press for home but only decaf since the colitis flare. Picking up his cup and laptop, he walked outside, sat at the table for two. Balzac probably disliked if not despised dogs, too busy writing, his time intensely his, life too short to interrupt with training a canine how to behave, particularly a house dog, a small dog like the Chihuahua-mix the size of their gray cat, fussy enough not to use the litter box unless completely clean. It was Tom's job to wash the bamboo floor and now with a second pet, the pup she wanted, he would have another infant to take care of.

Possibly that's why their friends with dogs found, in the animal's passing, their own life no longer leashed, not having to get up early to walk the dog or make it the last thing they did at night. Tom never entertained the thought that grief could keep them from another trip to the shelter.

But she, who did so little around the house now that his adjunct teaching at City College had evaporated, wanted to add to their tribe, tether him to a dog. Every night, every morning, every day scheduled around the pet's needs, time never to be recovered and what did they find in return, an animal licking between their toes, following them from room to room to be petted and hugged and tended to. This neediness, this emotional incubus was not what he desired. His cup almost empty and the crowd thinned, he looked toward the pet store four doors down and walked back into Starbucks ready to write.

Chapter 28

Adele constantly played the twenty-year game. Twenty years ago I was thirty, twenty years from now, I'll be seventy, counting years like a handful of coins, knowing they would be spent on trinkets, a pair of gold earrings or the mermaid wind chime sculpted from copper, its tail outlined in green with amethyst squiggles and silver glitter, a dream no doubt as all mermaids are but a tangible vision with a gold star in one hand and a blue shell in the other, and Adele held it in the breeze to catch the currents before hanging it on the ornamental apple tree outside their glass doors, an ageless woman with golden locks reminding Adele of the ballet dancers who hung in frames on her childhood wall, their forms perfect in pink, toe shoes never scuffed or dirtied, perpetually on point, waiting in this moment, unruffled by the past or future and later when she read "Ode on a Grecian Urn," she thought of her ballet dancers and how lovely they would look encircling any vase, almost touching hands, the audience on the edge of their seats, waiting for Gelsey Kirkland to reach out from the ceramic, alive and offering Adele a charm, a talisman for longevity, a silver marble almost an inch in diameter, that she placed in her left palm, and suddenly she felt the continuity of it all, how the urn and Gelsey and the mermaid met at the center, life converged, and there were no tears since existence was a sequence of bubbles, fragile and full of color, busting into another and though Adele could see them vanishing into the distant light, she felt they somehow would continually be, not in her sight or that of Tom or anyone else standing on earth now, but the bubbles were always somewhere always becoming something new because today, June 23, was the day she felt, for the first time truly felt, those she loved endlessly around her, leaving snatches of notes and crumpled tissues to remind Adele that time was arbitrary and depended on limited eyesight but existence continued forever to wrap her in its threads.

Chapter 29

Adele looked up from her laptop. "Caffeine may cramp creativity," she said.

"Really?"

"It says one's mind becomes too focused with caffeine, blocking creative thinking."

"Thought I wouldn't be able to write without it," Tom said, lifting the white cup of cold decaf coffee.

"In graduate school I felt I couldn't think seriously without a cigarette," Adele said.

"How long has it been?"

"Twenty-five years," she said, "and still thinking."

"Seriously?"

Adele ran her fingers through her hair. "Why do you always do that?"

"Do what?" Tom asked.

"Make me feel inadequate." Tom looked at her, reaching for her arm when Adele turned to face him.

"Come on, I was playing," he said.

"You're always playing."

"Don't be so touchy."

"You never say what you mean."

"I'm not the one who talks in circles."

"What do you mean?"

"Thursday you wanted me to stay home and not play golf."

"So?"

"You never told me. Only complained I don't pay attention to you and started crying."

Adele looked away, took a sip of coffee. "I remember the day your mom passed. Why don't you remember when Dad left?" she said.

"I don't remember much from that summer."

And how could he, ravaged by ulcerative colitis? He slept two or three hours each day and spent nights on the toilet as he spent most of his days. Fists slamming against the bathroom wall.

Adele started to choke up, going back to that dark summer when she thought both her dad and Tom were slipping away. Her dad in a nursing home, his eyes closed more than open. Tom at home, running from bed to toilet, his mind a fog. Adele squeezed his hand, thankful he was still beside her.

Chapter 30

Outside, dahlias drooped. Inside, he put fans in the windows and she sliced lemons. They shed clothes and drank sweet tea over ice.

"Is it too hot to make love?" Adele asked.

Tom leaned down and kissed the scar next to her right breast. When younger, she wore tight white T-shirts pulling them closer. Full of magic and ready, always ready. If his hand brushed them, they blushed. When he kissed them, they grew. Some days Tom wondered where he would be without them, their fullness, how he would be with what was left.

"Never," he said.

Chapter 31

Adele stood in front of the window, watching the puppy leap against the glass. She could walk inside, sanitize her hands, and pet the Chihuahua-mix as she'd done for the last five days, stroking his hair between jumps, seeing him curled in her lap, snuggled against her stomach. She read that the breed would easily attach to the family especially if the family were calm, easy-going. But sometimes, when left mostly with one person, the pup would bond fiercely, possessive of the chosen master, suspicious of others. A pack of two. Such a thought made her uneasy, almost sad. What if the pup became Tom's dog, slept on his knees, against his back, and identified with him because he was always the one there? She couldn't take the rejection, she wanted to be the one sought, the Chihuahua burrowing inside her, calling for her, always waiting for her. Tom seemed content with Gray and his independent emotions. She wanted more, some breathing love she could always hold. She would come back tomorrow, maybe there would be a sign, maybe the puppy would be gone.

Chapter 32

"Do you worry about death?" Adele squirmed on the couch and crossed her legs.

"Not really. I focus on what I have to do today," Tom said, laying aside his iBook and turning toward her. She was fifty, seven years older than he.

First of the month, sliver of a moon and Adele felt the night, closed in, couldn't see beyond the light in the TV room, suddenly her body flushed. The darkness didn't always alarm her. There were nights she'd lie on the bed, three pillows, knees tented, and read *Anna Karenina*, more satisfying that Adele hid her own worry in Levin's about Kitty and the land. But some nights Adele needed more than a novel, she wanted to hear a voice, Tom's voice, talking her though her anxiety, her almost irrational fear though tonight the presence of the dark seemed anything but irrational.

"Have I always been like this?" she asked, wanting to burrow in his arms.

"Like what?" he said and walked to the kitchen. "Want to split a beer?"

Tom's first answer to her unease. He knew Adele loved to split everything, halving was a ritual like communion, if we share our food, that's the beginning: we'll share our love, our interests, our life. With each year together Adele grew more dependent, saying they were like Plato's soul mates destined to find their other on earth though it took Tom and her more time to find their way through the mingling parts. But there he was in his jeans and white Oxford shirt, sleeves rolled up, hair like a Romantic poet, or so Adele thought, thick, curly and shoulder length.

Neither imagined his losing it, but like the rest of their lives, attrition became inevitable and one day she noticed a bald spot on his crown. It appeared suddenly, no warning, when they were in bed and she leaned over him, a circle the diameter of her thumb touching her index finger, and she was startled. "Tom, your hair is gone" as if the utterance was the cause, the curse, not that his uncle on one side and his grandfather on the other had any hair past fifty. But Tom, whose father died with his hair intact, was too young, still in jeans and an Oxford shirt so when Adele announced that November night he was losing hair the clock went askew, its hour hand flying from two to seven to twelve and around again and again, they could hear the clicking, the warning, the sign that life would be different now, minutes would turn into hours so quickly that months obscured days and years, well they just ran a marathon, blurring the past, and one November night

Adele leaned over Tom and there it was, the tell-tell promise that they would not be here forever, like their parents and their parents before them, Tom and Adele would join the fold edging closer to the cliff and if Tom and Adele were lucky, they'd be stopped in a stand of bamboo, giving them the time and space to take it all in, their life their love their loss, and slow down so they could enjoy each moment, each day without being buried in what will happen. But this night was not one of those moments. Tonight, in the dark, she was not safe from encroaching loss.

Chapter 33

That's what it was, yes, the sun, a trapezoid on her bamboo floor. She wasn't even sure if she knew what a trapezoid was, those days in geometry long ago, Mrs. Burgoyne in thick beige hose and a floral dress, exuding the mustiness of tobacco, and they stopped in their seats, held their breaths that Burgoyne would not single them out, ask for an answer, rapping the wooden desk with her nails. Yes, a trapezoid of light. Adele had remembered the shape after all those years, two parallel lines with uneven sides, the metal clothes rack on rollers, long shirts and short on plastic hangars waiting for someone to wash or iron or wear defined the side closest to the bed. Trapezoid. The sound, that's what she remembered most about eleventh grade math, all those delicious words—perpendicular, quadrilateral, rhombus, isosceles, especially isosceles with all the s's tickling her tongue. She would roll the syllables, listen to their sibilants whistle on ivory, and think of her new skates, the ones her mother bought at Loveman's Department Store three weeks before Christmas. She handed them to Adele that day, a white box with white skates so Adele could slice parallel lines. Though her marks were often ragged, splinters glistening under Loveman lights at the store's indoor rink, she dreamed of cutting the ice clean.

Had she outgrown those skates and skating, giving them up for boys with pimples and their sticky hands, grasping, reaching like the tentacles of some kraken, leaving marks jagged and uneven? All that fumbling and pushing when no meant no or maybe or yes.

Chapter 34

Adele spent some of her earlier life as a journalist, not full time for the *Miami Herald* or *Atlanta Journal-Constitution*. She freelanced for a woman, once the *Chicago Tribune* features editor, who provided "filler" for weekly and bi-weekly newspapers in the Midwest. Adele's last interviewee was a woman named Nancy, who survived a back-alley abortion in the days before Roe v Wade. After turning it in, Adele quit and became a telemarketer but kept a copy of the story.

Nancy at nineteen, given the phone number by a friend, called from a pay booth, afraid of being overheard in her apartment. *Wednesday at noon at the Daybreak Motel on Pine and Chester, $300.* Not too far a cab ride. She didn't mention the abortion to her boyfriend and went alone in her old slicker and jeans. Walked to the second floor, knocked, a woman in a white smock and white shoes asked her to sit in the chair. Naugahyde brown, two of them with a table and lamp between. The outdoor/indoor carpet nubby orange and tan, walls grammar school green with two double beds, above each was a sailboat on fake blue water in a plastic frame.

The nurse, or who Nancy assumed the woman in white to be, was in the bathroom running water, clanking utensils. No phone, no television, two arm chairs, two beds, two lamps and a desk with a folding chair. The room smelled of Clorox. Suddenly, the door opened, a man in black pants, a dress shirt with sleeves rolled up and no tie walked to the bathroom and back, looked down at Nancy, breathing bourbon fumes: *Take off your shoes, jeans and underwear, no screaming or I'll leave.*

She'd read about abortions, knew at her early stage, two months, the procedure should be scraping and that's it, not much pain, not much time. So why this warning?

The nurse pulled down the spread and Nancy lay on the top sheet, lumps beneath her, the mattress so cheap or old, she didn't know which, or maybe dying coals and this was her test of faith. The man in black sat in the folding chair at the end of the bed, taking the forceps and saying: *Don't Scream or I'll leave.* She felt something cold and hard scrape inside her. No sedative, no pain pills and all she could do was grind her teeth, try to hear waves washing against her belly, back and forth like magic fingers, the sun warming her shoulders when the voice said: *That's it, lie here thirty minutes and then if you feel woozy, the nurse can give you something.* The door slammed.

Chapter 35

Tom was sitting near the artificial Christmas tree untangling lights. As Adele squeezed by, her elbow hit a glass ornament that fell and exploded, red glass spread in an imperfect circle. This was their first Christmas in the new house they bought in Santa Barbara, their first Christmas without parents. Her father dying shortly after his mother last spring.

"Oooh."

He heard her and thought, she must be bleeding. Cut. But all he saw was her looking at the shattered ornament.

"Are you ok?" he asked.

"That was my dad's."

He tried not to sigh or say anything or make a gesture because he knew a storm might come and probably he would be implicated by thought or deed or lack thereof. He stood and carried the lights to the kitchen table. When he came back, she was sitting beside the broken ornament, staring at it.

"Do you even miss your mother?" she asked.

He sat down across from her counting out Mississippis. "Of course, I miss her." And he did miss his mother decorating every room of the house with tinsel and bells and baking cheese straws, hiding them until Christmas Eve.

"Why don't you ever talk about her?" Adele asked

"I do sometimes, but she's gone. It always comes to that," he said. He remembered shortening phone calls and visiting less often after his father died, leaving his mother too much to her own choices. Couldn't understand her needs.

"Do you want to forget?" Adele asked, looking at him as if he should say something more, do something. The way he should have done something for his mother.

"Are you warm?" Tom asked. He opened the sliding glass door and picked a chocolate, the pound box on the coffee table, waiting to be emptied. He sat next to her this time. "We have our lives, you and me. We have tomorrow."

Adele pushed the glass fragments into a neat circle, then a smaller circle, and an even smaller circle. Glass dust stuck to her fingers reflecting light.

Tom left her to get the dustpan and broom.

Chapter 36

Adele thought of the conversation where Ana went silent and then blurted, "Something has bothered me a long time and I can't hold it back."

"What?"

"When we first met, you said we must remember each other's birthdays if we were going to be friends."

"I said that?" Such a comment seemed so uncharacteristic of Adele whose value of behavior between friends didn't include recognizing anyone's day of birth especially her own.

"Yes, and I've always sent an email or called you. But you never remember mine," she said.

"I'm so sorry, Ana. I don't even recall saying anything about birthdays."

"Well, you did. And birthdays become more important as we get older."

While Adele was unconcerned about birth rituals, she was obsessed with the passage of time, understood each day as a gift, turning yesterday, perhaps, into a missed occasion, and they'd begun to talk of life in terms of the years left to create, what they wanted to accomplish. Ana wanted to publish her novel about Serbia, thirty years in the writing. Adele wasn't as sure about a specific end though she'd just finished *Talking Did Not Come Easily to Diana*, a flash novella about an adjunct teaching English at a California Community College. And Adele knew she must continue to write, tell her story, changing as the light changes any given moment.

The morning trapezoid shrinking toward afternoon.

Chapter 37

To save Gray from evergreen toxins, Adele and Tom had bought an artificial Christmas tree. Red-blue-yellow-green lights flashed day and night, bewitching them by New Year's Eve. February she purchased red construction paper and cut out hearts. Two-inch diameters suspended limb to limb with ribbon.

Gray slept beneath.

Over a bottle of Syrah, they sat on the couch facing the tree.

"Should we take it down?" he asked.

"It would be cruel to dismantle in April," she said. "Imagine bunnies and eggs."

"I can't," he said. "I'm still on hearts."

They watched the lights the hearts the sleeping cat, knowing spring would come and they could be sitting there, watching the lights the hearts the sleeping cat.

Chapter 38

Three weeks until the deadline of the SoCal Festival for One-Act Plays. Tom was revising *Almost a Day*, spending the mornings cutting stage direction and editing dialogue. But this morning he felt the difference in Adele's silence as she held her cup of coffee, looking out at the plastic flamingoes, some fallen from their stilts, bodies broken, pink pieces lying wounded among the flowers.

"What's wrong?" Tom asked.

"I'm sad," Adele said.

"Anything I can do?" Tom asked.

"No," she replied. He lifted his messenger bag, feeling the heft of his laptop, the play, reading glasses and headphones. Also *The Collected Works of Lydia Davis* if he felt the need for a longer absence.

His favorite table by the window was taken, but the woman didn't look like she had come to stay. Only a muffin and *The Santa Barbara News* with her coffee. Maybe the yappy dog tied to the table outside was hers. Why bring it along only to abandon it? Tom set up his computer and began condensing the play, trying to hear the voices of different actors only to hear Adele say I'm fine. She didn't lie well. But what could he do except listen to her repeat the same complaints about the inevitability of aging and death and disappointment. Longing to be young.

Tom began to write as the voices of his characters finally drowned out Adele's voice.

Chapter 39

When it rains in Santa Barbara, they hold their breath and stay inside unless absolutely necessary. Under a black raincoat Adele left the house. She had a poetry class to teach at City College where parking lots would be filling with pools of water and students driving 50 on the 101, water running down windshields and spilling over curbs. The weather channel predicted three inches. Visions of La Conchita cottages in mudslide terracotta 2005—roof monuments to the dead. More cottages rose from the earth shortly thereafter to dare another deluge to bring them down. Fire and Rain, Rain and Fire. Frost got it wrong for them, for Californians on the Pacific looking into the Santa Ynez Mountain chaparral, child of *chapparo*: dwarf evergreen raised in a wet winter and scorching summer. Warm welcoming shrub when offshore winds blow dry and hot.

Chapter 40

Some weeks he made pizza from scratch with fresh mozzarella, tomatoes, and basil sprinkled with virgin oil on a papery crust. Tom uncorked a Zinfandel and called her to the table. Some weeks when his colitis flared, he ate applesauce and farmer's cheese, toast and boiled potatoes. No wine, red or white. His colon was enraged during earthquakes, tsunamis, and radiation leaks. His horoscope predicted upheaval: Mars conjunct with Uranus, the planet of surprises.

"Are you frightened?" Adele asked.

"Of course. I don't want a colectomy, my asshole in the middle of my stomach."

Through the sliding glass doors Tom studied a crow iridescent black picking the grass for seed, short beak up and down like a desk ornament. She watched too, the breeze cooling their silence.

"That won't happen," she said.

"The drugs aren't working," he said.

"Did you ever hear the Aesop story about the crow and the pitcher?"

"Remind me."

"A thirsty crow comes across a pitcher with water at the bottom," she said. "Tries to reach the water with her beak. She can't. Tries to push the pitcher over. She can't. Then drops pebbles, one by one, into the water until it rises high enough to drink."

"What the fuck are you talking about?"

Chapter 41

His father wearing a tweed hat sitting on a dry stone wall in the Cotswolds, his last trip to England. Tom kept the picture, one of the few, always on his desk, and occasionally stopped to look at his father's dark eyes and dark hair. A textile salesman traveling the East Coast during the week, home most Fridays and off again Monday morning.

He didn't spend much time with Tom as a kid and when he turned thirty and his father had open heart surgery and Tom knew days may be limited so did his father, the night before saying he wished he'd been home more. From then on, they believed in borrowed time. In graduate school at Ohio State, Tom came home weekends to be with him. As some men remember football Saturdays with Dad, Tom remembered sitting on the couch, watching Julia Child and Justin Wilson, then shopping at The West Side Market and cooking, standing in the kitchen with a glass of Cote du Rhone.

"What would your mother think of us?" Tom's father asked.

"Lazy and no good."

They laughed, and Tom heard the unrestrained sound of youth, that careless noise rising somewhere in the belly and creating undulating motion, young men in sleeves rolled up and women in fan skirts, martini in hand, moving in and out of the kitchen while Tom in footed pajamas watched the behavior of adults, lips leaving red half moons on glasses and dangling black and silver cigarette holders, wanting to be Audrey Hepburn before they knew what skin and bones really meant and Cary Grant winding through the beautiful men and women, never neglecting one for the other.

And Tom looked at his dad taking another sip and wanted to hug him, wrap his arms around his chest and tell him it was all right, he was the father Tom wanted, the man who spent his waning hours talking with his son. After his father passed, Tom took some of his father's clothes. His shirts were too short, his shoes and hats too large. The ties, of course, fit though Tom rarely wore ties.

Chapter 42

An errant hummingbird sliced air, zooming up then hovering around each red-tubed flower. The other rose-pink throat attacked and chased it off. Gray froze like a sphinx on his haunches behind the French door, watching every move of the birds he'd never catch. His soft cries of desire reverberating off the glass. Adele in the burgundy La-Z-Boy was still in her nightshirt while Tom at the Farmer's Market gathered heirloom tomatoes and spring onions, celery and carrots, all local, all on a list they made together.

She sometimes imagined herself a recluse, a hermit, holed up in their house with Tom and Gray, her books and the computer, looking at the outside world safely from within, thinking the great adventure was not flying to Argentina or climbing Annapurna but dropping into her own psyche, excavating her fears, spreading them in the sun so she could understand how her father's slaps never faded through time, how she couldn't forget but could almost forgive. Her father, strong into his nineties, tall and lean, calling her baby, forgetting the bruises, even denying them.

The day he died, she heard him speak her name, and woke Tom. It was 3 a.m. Six hours later her brother called from Alabama. "Dad doesn't have long."

Chapter 43

Most July mornings Santa Barbara was covered in fog from the Pacific, hiding the sun, blocking the heat, low 60s, unlike Alabama mornings, heat rising before breakfast, shutting many folk behind air-conditioned doors. Adele didn't miss those stifling summers, daring mosquitoes to bite unless doused in Off under long sleeves and jeans, armor against the blood-sucking female, antennae detecting seventy-two types of odor, particularly smell emitting carbon dioxide, human sweat at dawn or dusk.

Vampiric insect whose labium enfolds her mouthparts as she probes her host for vessels, routes of red protein, and when she finds them will bend into a bow before unsheathing her mandibles and maxillae, her head moving back and forth, her arrows piercing deeper into the skin for blood, food for her eggs. Bumps rose on Adele's ankle.

Chapter 44

Adele's first teaching job after grad school was at Warren College on a one-year contract, teaching women's lit and writing. Still new to the classroom, she couldn't believe she was being paid to do what she loved, at night lying in bed, thinking about Woolf's "A Haunted House," how she would start by asking students to write about their favorite ghost story then form a big circle for the question "How is Woolf's house haunted?" Playing with images, passing around a crystal ball, flawless sphere where the students might see the apple in the loft, through the windowpane, or in the drawing room turning its yellow side. This was interpretation, looking into the nature of imagination, holding it in their hands, entering its skewed space, the heat shaping their vision, shared with the rest of the class. And Adele would listen, their sibilants harsh then hushed, a stream of air falling at the teeth's sharp edge.

Twenty years later, tenured and promoted, Adele still felt a thrill in September, shuffling assignments on the syllabi, adding a new novel to the

Brit Lit survey, the first night exhilaration walking into a sea of faces, some new, some returning, a line at the door to add the class. This was the beginning of a sixteen-week journey together, from *Beowulf* through Behn, through stacks of essays and tests until that final day she would breathe deeply, looking ahead at winter break, five weeks of solitude, holing up in her house with the books she wanted to read, writing what she wanted to write. She had begun to question what she once claimed: her teaching nourished her writing. Was she ready to step away from students, her time always being her own, no office visits, no nights grading, no appointed hours to perform?

To be a professor had been one of her dreams since college and now to think of her life without teaching, without being sought by students, calling her Doc. An informal, almost affectionate title with enough suggestion to let them know she had done it, received her Ph.D. when many of her classmates never finished their dissertations. So much of her being defined by it all and to give it all up, to leave students waiting outside another professor's door, even the thought of not being there saddened her, emptied her of meaning, for she was a teacher, the very person she longed to be, someone her dad introduced as "This is my daughter. She teaches at City College," and every time he said that, she felt something warm spread though her body, the joy she experienced because her father, the dad who grew up in a coal mine and struggled for a college degree, announced her to the world as his daughter, the professor.

She wondered if she would be standing at a white board and just vanish into its space or would she begin to feel the pressure of ungraded essays more than the delight of being there and know then it was time.

Chapter 45

Adele thought about Elizabeth Hardwick, how she moved from Lexington, Kentucky to New York City, going back south for family visits, never feeling at home there, always the outsider. "The stain of place," she called it, dirty marks not easily washed, physical blemish like the jagged scar in the palm of Adele's right hand ripped scaling over barbed wire, running from a car of boys at the Marshal Drive-In. She was making out in the back seat with Tony when three of his buddies crawled in the front and Olivia Newton John pierced the dark with "You're the One That I Want." Adele grabbed the door handle, escaping to endure three more years of high school, sitting on wooden bleachers in PE, Mrs. Green saying abstinence was the only birth control. Adele knew otherwise. She wondered how she could love her mother and father so much but feel trapped in a time capsule where Jim Crow thrived and nice white girls attended business school, any day catching a nice white boy from college. Adele refused to take typing or home management or babysit for the

Taylors next door because she knew it was all a sham to cheat her out of her birthright, to sabotage her brain, fitting her for the role of some Stepford wife. A pretty little dummy baking apple pies in pinafore dresses and spreading her legs for the man of the house, pumping out babies at his whim, and wiping every surface white.

Chapter 46

Her mother's lamp, white porcelain with eight sides, two front and back cornered with three sides about two inches each. Bronze, yellow and brown zinnias curl around a bluebird flying through. Adele's mother was a woman of the fifties and sixties, a lady never walking with a cigarette, always writing thank you notes even in her last days, and never missed the birthday of family or friends. Quite the looker too, blonde hair and a Hollywood smile, full lips and straight teeth. She died young, fifty-five, before Adele was old enough to work out the kinks, still at war with her mother's plans for her—colonial home for parties spilling onto the lawn and kids in white starched dresses and shorts, a lavish life her mother had wanted instead of living in an Appalachian town, rows of cotton and tomatoes. And Adele did want more—to leave Sand Mountain as soon as she finished high school and put the past behind, discover what lay beyond the state line and the next line. At eighteen she made it as far as the University of Florida, not Goucher College where she wanted to go, but her parents, especially her mother, felt that Adele needed boys around her and never lost the chance to tell her so.

Questions began in ninth grade.

"Aren't you interested in boys?" her mother asked, taking Adele's glasses off her face.

"Not really," Adele said, putting them back on and looking at the porcelain lamp, wondering why her mother cared.

"Why?"

"Why not? They're boring. Only interested in getting to second base," Adele said. "I have other things to do."

"Like homework," her mother lifted Adele's red Civics book and flipped though it as if the words didn't exist, only the paper, and paper was available everywhere.

Adele stood up.

"Sit down, young lady. I'm not through."

"Mom, why don't you like me studying?"

"Because that's all you do," her mother said. "When I was your age, I had a steady boyfriend. Jimmy Lockhart, eight years older."

Adele shifted on the couch, her butt going to sleep.

"You better wake up, Miss Four Eyes."

And the questions continued regularly, precisely until Adele was a junior in college and confessed to her mother that she slept with an Alpha Tau Omega during spring break, a lie that triggered a new set of questions.

Chapter 47

Sunset and evening star. Blood-red and flaxen fan into twilight. *And one clear call for me.* She stared at her father's wide smile and her mother's long legs in the photograph. Between them Adele swung, eyes closed and her hands holding theirs. A voice was heard saying—you are silhouettes on sand. Adele confessed to her father: "I was afraid you and mother would fall asleep and leave me in the dark."

He smiled wider than the fading daylight. "You were a girl then. Nothing worse could happen. Now you are a woman."

Chapter 48

She laid her hand over the puffed ridge around the scar, tracks tracing a sphere cut from the bone, once an orb of light lifting her blouse, inviting Tom to come toward her, complete. She'd seen a veteran interviewed on TV by Montel Williams. "My left arm throbs whenever the weather changes even though some sniper blew it off more than ten years ago," he said. "The ghost won't leave me alone." Then the veteran froze. His image broken into squares and rectangles. Vowels evaporated, left consonants behind, useless.

Adele flipped to another station. Every day she felt her skin burning. Everybody who saw it was transfixed by their own reflection. She told Tom that the surgeon placed her breast in a bell jar at University Hospital. She signed the forms, releasing them, not really understanding. She just wanted the breast gone, away. Not caring what was done with it.

Tom imagined a young woman who had always wanted one like Adele's waiting outside the operating room. Holding a box. Ready to take it home. Willing to risk it.

Chapter 49

One could never know Adele, not really, for she often wore black leggings and a ruche blouse, ruche a French word for beehive, the pleats and flutes giving her a vintage look, someone who slipped into the bistro while the couple in back danced to Piaf, and Adele, alone, sat at the far left table next to the window, ordered a decaf espresso, midnight close and she no longer drank cabernet, wondering if life would ever be the party it once was for how can you be joyous, speak of Marianne jumping into the fountain with the two cement dolphins side by side spewing water, splashing into the cistern with nothing but a flute of Moet, and Mia leaving the Palace Grill not before stopping at the door, too late for the hostess, and picking up the Phalaenopsis orchid, fleshy purple petals spread like a moth in flight, its trajectory the candle almost melted. Adele sipped her coffee, asking for a plain profiterole, the cream sweet, raising her spirits, recalling walks amid the Birds of Paradise, green beak, tuft of yellow flowers and she turned to a solitary stem of fuchsia and picked it, just one, to show Tom that she had been out that day, away from her books, immersing herself in the earth, and when she offered him the flower, he took the Venetian blue vase, once his mother's, from the sideboard and placed the bloom in the glass, pouring water to keep its blossom alive.

Chapter 50

Adele felt scared even thinking about Tuesday morning. Tom was awake two hours before her, unloaded the dishwasher, pushed the garbage cans to the curb, ate his yogurt and trail mix and took fifty milligrams of prednisone and one Benadryl prepping for his Remicade infusion—the medicine that had kept his colitis manageable for the last two years.

She was on her first cup of coffee, checking email when Tom said he had "come over tired" and was going to nap. Nothing else. He walked into the bedroom, lay down and was asleep. An hour later she shook his shoulders without any response. Adele pulled him to a sitting position, he opened his eyes and looked as if he didn't see her. When she stood him up, he took a stumbling run into the wall. She caught him around the waist and he turned, walked to the bathroom and urinated. "Tom, say something. What's going on?" He stumbled to the sink, took the toothpaste in his left hand and twisted the cap for what seemed like two minutes. Something bad was happening, something she couldn't handle alone. He didn't see her. He didn't hear her. While he fumbled with the tube, she called 911.

Two hours later Tom was in a blue and white hospital gown on a bed in Cottage Hospital Emergency Room. Sleeping. The ER doctor woke him up, more easily than she did, and asked a few questions. What's your name?

Tom looked at the doctor, minutes slowing down before he said, "Tom."

Where are you?

Again, time lapsed when Tom said "Not sure, maybe a hospital."

What's the date? More accumulating seconds, Tom's head down, his customary posture when thinking about his response, "July 17."

The doctor asked him to walk. Tom was steady enough for the doctor to say "No signs of a stroke." Tom went back to sleep.

Dr. ER returned. "All the blood work and tests are normal. Must be a pharmaceutical issue." He roused Tom, then said to Adele, "He only needs to sleep it off. You can take him home when the paper work's done."

More than six hours, they were in that room. The screen flickered Tom's pulse and blood pressure in red and green. An occasional attendant stuck his head through the curtain, and a nurse came in once to arrange Tom's pillow.

When they got home, Tom slept. Adele woke him three hours later. This time it was easy. She shook his shoulder and his eyes opened. But the day was lost. He remembered lying down in his bed at 9:30 that morning and waking up at 9:00 that night. On his chest, two brass nipples the nurse forgot to remove.

Chapter 51

Tom couldn't shake the horror of losing twelve hours, lying down for a nap and waking in the same spot almost half a day later, Adele's hand on his shoulder. She leaned down, kissed his forehead, and asked what he remembered then sketched the events from 911 to six hours in ER. Tom had a foggy vision of tubes in his hands and nothing else till he woke that night. His internist had ordered an **MRI** for his brain, to be sure, to rule out a stroke, and mentioned a mass might trigger deep sleep but didn't expect to find anything like that. "No, don't worry." That's all Tom could do, constantly checking the Mayo Clinic website. MS, tumor, aneurysm, stroke. MRIs look for them but Tom had no symptoms, no confusion or headaches, no blurred sight or stammering speech.

He imagined an anomaly, a mutation of already mutated cells, a blob suffocating his cerebral matter, moving counter clockwise from the temporal to the frontal lobe, stealthily, without interference of walking or hearing as lost hours become days, weeks become months when Tom will take a nap and wake Rip Van Winkle, Adele gone, his beard a foot long, his iPad rotted, his house choked in dust, and the front yard a jungle. He will walk through palms and pines into a clearing, see black pods on stilts and smart cars running on raised rails, only to wonder what happened.

Chapter 52

Two weeks before fall semester, the dreams began. Adele was teaching composition in a banquet hall packed with older students, her parents' age, eight per round table, speaking aloud while she gave directions. Two women to the right kept talking, slate letters falling out of their mouths, pings rose into thuds as more women stood in clusters, their voices sounded above Adele's, shards of the alphabet flew shoulder high, ballistic, moved under their own momentum and the force of gravity, reversing their trajectory, pulling them downward toward Adele, her jeans no armor against the attack of thousands of flint splinters aimed at her, almost touching her denim when she closed her eyes, opening them on a shore of smoothed pebbles, searching for a flat one the size of a half-dollar to skip across the water the way her dad taught her, holding the slick stone between her right thumb and forefinger, swinging her arm back and horizontal to her thigh. The angle of toss was important since the trailing rock would breach the water first, jump upward and leap across the surface, slowing down with each bounce.

Chapter 53

Adele read *Big Sur* and wanted to hike the spiritual wilderness of Kerouac before and after the hero left his shell, barely getting through breakfast when he saw faces pressed against the window, hands reaching for his shirt. What did they want, those pasty-eyed kids, driving down from San Francisco? The army doctor called it precocious madness and kicked him out. Kerouac did what many of us writers do when life stinks and we want to exorcize whatever has us in its talons, dragging nails down our back, blood in channels deeper than life, running through our past and future. We start writing. He'd paste together paper so he could feed one lone sheet through his typewriter, drinking whiskey and malt liquor to keep going.

Adele thought alcohol and drugs an overly wrought trapping but she felt the gnawing, the desire to lose her conscious self always beating against her heart, ringing in her ears. Sometimes she couldn't bear the loss in life, her niece, her father, herself, and would lock the door, grab the headphones and computer, staring at a blank page like staring at those pictures long enough to see another emerge, a palimpsest not there when she sat down and she'd fall into the whiteness, the immensity of it all until she felt whole again, or close to whole, when the words began appearing and grounded her to something more, something beyond her sadness, something she could call home.

Chapter 54

A man with a wild shock of white hair was riding his bike in Elings Park, his cardigan barely enough to break the breeze. In her light ski jacket, Adele sat on the stone bench to watch the fog rise over the cliff. Einstein rode past the bench then began to circle round and round. After the third orbit the sun broke through, pushing away the fog, and he was gone.

"What do you make of that dream?" Tom asked.

"I saw a picture of Einstein riding a bike in Santa Barbara at the home of Ben Meyer."

"Who is Ben Meyer?"

"I googled him and several popped up. But the one with Einstein was a Caltech trustee who lived here. Einstein visited Caltech three times in the early 1930s and left the school a legacy in projects on relativity," Adele said.

"Do you understand $E=mc2$?"

"I know E is energy, m is mass, and c is the

speed of light. That light can be measured in particles and waves."

"What did the man of light say to you?"

"If you see the Buddha on the road, kill it."

"Wasn't Einstein Jewish?"

"It doesn't matter," Adele said. "I'm Buddhist."

Chapter 55

Tom sat at the round kitchen table reading *Blood Meridian* for the third time. Adele placed slices of orange in front of him.

"Have you finished *Mrs. Dalloway*?" she asked.

There was a pause, always a felt presence between her questions and his responses, longer now that he wasn't teaching. Finally, he looked up, the novel still open.

"Almost." And looked down again, turning the page.

How could he say so little, almost, and that was it, that was all. He had lived with her fifteen years, he knew she adored Woolf, especially Clarissa, and all he could say was almost, one word as if it were enough.

Wanting to scream, Adele stood nearly twenty seconds, her hands squeezing the rail of the chair before she sat across from him. He mumbled or she thought he mumbled and his carriage hardened because he sensed what was coming

"What do you think?" she asked.

He breathed in this deliberate manner that bordered on a groan.

"It's a bit slow. The writing is lovely but Woolf doesn't pull me in," he said, his finger holding his place in McCarthy.

Lovely. She wanted to hit him. She wanted to talk about how the novel slips from the present to the past and back again, how everyone has a point of view even the girl selling petticoats, how the miracle of existence culminates in Clarissa at the top of the stairs.

He could see her lips tightening, her presence receding. Closing his novel, he said, "Sorry. That was a bit glib. The language is pure as one image unfolds into another. But she reads like a performance, a spectacle." He pushed his chair back so he could cross his legs.

"Spectacle?" she asked. "What the hell do you mean? You read about massacre and bloodshed and then call Woolf spectacle because Woolf's not killing for her audience's attention."

"Woolf killed Septimus," he said.

"Asshole."

He knew enough not to smile. Adele walked to the fridge and grabbed a bottle of water; maybe she'd throw it at him or shatter the glass and stab him. On the walnut coffee table they bought at a garage sale in Ventura was the most recent *Harper's*, which reports that a team of forensic engineers at The University of Leicester measured the amount of force used in bottle stabbings and called it effectively phenomenal. She twisted the cap off the bottle and sat down across from Tom.

"God. I want to hit you," she said.

Closing the novel again, he looked up at her and scratched his cheek, waiting.

"Ever hit a woman?" she asked.

"Does my sister count?"

"No."

She drank some water. The fridge started up and she turned and watched it before looking back at him. Why does he always have to be a smartass? He's so good at so much. But his silence hurts, leaves me feeling stranded. (Long before they met, her then boyfriend and she started drinking Bloody Marys at Myrtle Beach in the early afternoon. She woke with a splitting headache, nose swollen and raccoon eyes. X-rays showed no skull fracture. Adele told everyone she fell on the pier. The boyfriend bought her roses.)

Tom pushed the novel away, still staring at her.

"I've never slapped a woman," he said, "though sometimes I've wanted to. But I feel guilty enough."

Chapter 56

The next morning he watched her pajamas cling to her ass, strong and tight like a runner, muscular in the right places. She was quiet, almost timid, waking to her own rhythm as she liked to say. He was the one usually up early, particularly since his colitis, read *The New York Times* on his iPad in the bathroom, and fed the cat while she slept on.

Ever hit a woman? It wasn't her question that surprised him yesterday. He knew she had dark holes like his, remorse she kept hidden. But the lie startled him. I've never slapped a woman though sometimes I've wanted to. He had. Why was he afraid to tell her? Did he want her to think him incapable of violence?

Once between the marriages, he slapped a woman so hard the skin around her hip turned purple. But the woman said, do it, harder you prick, and he did but only where no one would see, her stomach, her ass. That night Tom yielded to something he had always fantasized, doing what the woman wanted, possibly more. And the following day, he was sick, not just from too much booze, he always cured that with a can of coke and a couple of aspirin. But he felt used up as if he had consumed part of himself.

The bathroom door scraped the tile, slightly, and he feigned sleep. Adele slipped into bed. He felt her press against his back. He rolled over. Ready.

Chapter 57

The bay window had mint green curtains, tasseled ropes holding them apart, and wooden shutters opening onto Washington Square in San Francisco. Carved into the cherry headboard were vines and leaves. The bed, small, barely containing their bodies, more developed since they first slept together on a single mattress with no frame in his apartment. Young then and weighted by hope, they held to each other, her right arm over his chest, his arm over hers. Nothing was too compact. Under a sheet, their warmth filling the space. When she turned over, he turned and draped his left arm over her, breathing against her neck. If she woke early and closed the blinds, he might keep his place, content with her shape pressed into the sheets. Outside, in the park, women and men practiced tai chi, lifting their arms with one palm open.

Chapter 58

Tom liked these nights when Adele was teaching and he was alone. He'd retreat to his study—books everywhere. Stuffed into corners, scattered beneath his glass desk and stacked on the window ledge. He preferred more order and used to arrange them alphabetically, keeping a file of those read and when and his evaluation. But it all changed with Adele and negotiating space with someone who thought every surface begged to be covered and told Tom it was like the cliché. Nature fills a vacuum or abhors a vacuum. She was bad with words passed down, always altering them, refining, forgetting. When they met, her dining table was piled with bills and magazines and student essays and she said meals were to be eaten on the run and in front of the TV.

Tom was quiet and rarely disagreed and she seemed to like that about him. Then silence became an issue. Control a bigger issue. One October night Tom was reading and Adele had finished grading and she glared at him until he put down his novel, Edward P.

Jones' *The Unknown World.* She accused him of shutting her out and he watched her eyes become wet and she told him to say something. Anything. Don't sit there staring. He said he was thinking and she cried and he handed her a Kleenex. Now Tom was safe inside his world and wrote about how he felt manipulated by her, changing the characters and setting. Much of the time together, maybe most. Yet he knew he was more content with her than without. But her crying, her obsession with the past wore him out. Always questioning, accusing him of being blocked. Adele an open faucet, running and gushing. He checked the time and wrote for another two hours. Then Adele would be home and he would be cooking and listening.

Chapter 59

"It will get worse," Tom said as he rinsed a bread knife under the faucet. "Soon our friends will be dying."

"It frightens me. I adored Aunt Jan. Her shoulder-length brown hair, violet eyes, laughter vibrating the room."

"What else do you remember?" he asked.

"She exuded everything positive. Like the time she broke her back thrown from a horse. She said the injury gave her space to read."

"Concentrate on that," he said and sat at the glass table with a coffee mug advertising Café Du Monde.

"You're right, I know you're right," she said and stole a sip. "But Aunt Jan's eyes were empty. She talked to me as if I were my mom."

"You handled it well," Tom said. "Just went along with being your mom at that point. How much fun you had at the circus."

"That's what I did with Dad. When he saw girls swinging in trees, I asked him to describe them. Sometimes young with long black hair, at other times in floral dresses flying over their backs." Adele reached for a Kleenex.

"Defense mechanism?"

"Aunt Jan's thinking she was on a cruise was preferable to being in a nursing home," Adele said. "Who wouldn't rather be on a luxury ship to the Caribbean?"

Tom looked at his watch. It was one o'clock, another two hours before the funeral. Every loss was that much harder for Adele, but today she seemed in better spirits, even thought of speaking at the service, maybe read Jane Kenyon's "Let Evening Come."

> *Let it come, as it will, and don't*
> *Be afraid. God does not leave us*
> *Comfortless, so let evening come.*

Chapter 60

Tom carried the empty laundry basket into the bedroom. Adele propped up against the headboard with her laptop raised on her knees.

"I got another email from my student Lou," Adele said.

Tom filled the basket with black T-shirts, socks, and jeans—the staples of his wardrobe. "On schedule," he said and added a pair of brown corduroys and left the room as Adele began to read the email. All he heard was "Adele would you and Tom." Tom put the dirty clothes in the washer, made a shot of decaf espresso and walked back to the bedroom.

"Why do you leave the room when I'm talking?" she asked.

"I don't."

"You just did."

"I needed to get the laundry started and why do you start reading me an email when I'm doing chores?"

"Can't they wait?" Her hands deserted the keyboard and folded across her chest.

"Adele, everything here waits for you."

"What do you mean?"

"Just that. You want me to stop whatever I'm doing to listen to an email from a student," he said. "Why don't you ask when I'm not busy? An email from Lou could wait."

"You're always busy."

"I'm not your personal assistant."

"Then what are you?"

Tom fought his urge to leave, to swear, to throw something. Instead, he finished his coffee and set the glass carefully on the brass jewelry box on Adele's dresser.

"I could get a nine to five, but you would have to do half the chores and I wouldn't be able to help you with your classes." Tom said. "And I wouldn't be here to listen to Lou's fucking emails."

"I need some help here. I want your opinion on how to handle things. Even Lou."

"Do you think I'm a deadbeat?"

"Not really. Except when you leave for golf and I'm working on *Beowulf.* That bothers me. What about teaching adjunct again?"

"After how the school treated me during my colitis?" Tom said.

"You're right. I know you're right, but I'm jealous."

"Of me? Always defending why I don't work? I know how your colleagues think. Your family."

"Tom, forget them."

"Sometimes I feel you think the same."

"I don't." Adele said. "I used to wish you still taught but that's changed." She walked over and touched his arm, the soft way she did when they made love, her fingers lightly rubbing his skin before he says it tickles. Now he stepped back, turned his face toward the hall.

"You do so much to help me with classes," she said. "140 students would be unbearable without you reading some of their stuff."

"So why do you keep asking me the same question?" He walked out of the room, one of his machines sounding its alarm.

Chapter 61

Side by side on the love seat recliners, Adele and Tom fell deeper into silence until their thoughts lost the shape of words and she closed *Mrs. Dalloway*, laying her hand on his thigh. He turned and smiled, following her into the back room, avocado leaves scraping against the window and just enough afternoon light.

They still undressed each other. She slid his T-shirt off his shoulders into a soft heap and he slipped her shirt over her head down her back. She loved its tickle. The shedding of layers that hold them apart before lying together on cool sheets, wrapped in arms that know.

Chapter 62

Adele thought much about her mother, dead almost thirty years, some days feeling closer to her now than then. They had been so different when Adele was a girl, trying to find herself in a country split by Viet Nam and Nixon paranoia. Whatever her mom wanted like a well-mannered daughter with well-dressed grandchildren triggered an opposing desire in Adele. She wanted to be herself (whatever that meant), but she knew she had to dig and search for a meaning that fit her, not her mother, not her father. And Adele left Alabama for Florida then Illinois before settling, temporarily, in South Carolina.

Eight hours from her parents, she studied Woolf and Joyce, Johnson and Burney, holing up in the library cubicles at the University, closing out the world until her mother called one night and told Adele she had bone cancer but was in no pain. The doctor said she had "three fairly comfortable years."

Adele sobbed.

Chapter 63

One spring night Adele felt something hard, almost the size of a robin's egg, in her left breast. For two weeks her fingers returned to the unyielding lump, but only in the dark and after Tom started snoring. She would lie awake, thinking of the times her mother threw up before chemo and finally said, "Enough." Adele believed her mother devout until the oncologist named the cancer. No more church suppers or Sunday schools.

Ana called. "I'm pregnant. Pumping all those hormones into my body worked."

"How far along?" Adele asked.

"Almost two months and chanting."

Ana had been pregnant before, and with each miscarriage blamed herself. Calling in tears, "I'm a crone, my eggs are old."

Adele was older than Ana (in that nether land between sister and mother like a young college teacher) and used to imagine having a daughter she could teach to make origami rabbits and walk with to Shoreline

Park. But like those women waiting for their morning Pergonal, Adele was afraid. Afraid the doctors could not kill what was inside her, swimming through her, searching for a new place to settle and grow.

She looked at the bedside clock, her fingertips parting her hair, reading her scalp.

Chapter 64

Santa Barbara got hot March 27. No one could deny that. Women were wearing shorts to lunch at the Via Vai, some shorter than others depending on weight and age. Men wore shorts too but with them it was all about the heat. Nothing else. She had on Bermudas, he walking shorts, following the sun to a corner table under an umbrella, green canvas, green everything after seven days of rain. The waiter was not Italian, not cordial, probably new. Didn't pull out her chair. She took the view of the mountains leaving Tom the view of her. They ordered, per usual.

"Insulate Caprese, no basil," Adele said.

"Pizza Margherita," Tom said.

"Wine?" the waiter asked.

"A carafe of your house red," she said.

"A pitcher of water with lemon," Tom said.

The waiter left only the hint of a nod of understanding.

Adele and Tom talked about the waiter, declaring never to be apathetic but then, not before then, she shut her eyes, wandering through weeks of indifference, mocking his stomach problems, demanding his attention. She felt her pores closing, her pupils contracting, and he stared into her dark glasses, seeing himself faintly reflected in her lenses, receding.

"Let's start over," Adele said.

"What?" Tom said.

"The two of us, at a table, outside, under an umbrella, for the first time."

Chapter 65

16 June 2013
Santa Barbara, CA

Dear Ana,

Hope you're doing well. I could have sent an email, as we usually do, but I thought what I wanted to say needed its own letter tucked and sealed in an envelope. I probably should have written three months ago, but I've gone back and forth about whether to mention it to you for I don't think you consciously meant to hurt me, and it's taken this long to decide whether I should keep quiet or tell you. I'm writing this because I value your friendship and believe you value mine. I remember those months going through chemo and you called every day, being there to talk, to listen to my pains, to affirm life. And I loved you even more for not turning away and facing breast cancer with me.

But your comments about the Diana prose left me in complete disbelief. "Who cares about an adjunct teacher in California? The South is so much more interesting, inherently tragic." Even if you feel that way, why did you say it? Why not give me some advice on how to strengthen the piece? I've never said, and hope I never do say, "who cares" about any of your work. We write what we write, what we feel at that moment, and our words are unique at any given point. But yours stunned me, made me wonder if somehow I had weakened my voice, turned away from what I knew best. I take what you say to heart and feel torn, in this case, between listening to you or to myself. I think the South will always be a part of my voice whether I'm writing about tension with my dad or Diana's tension with her colleagues.

I want our friendship to stay strong and open, continue to age well as we hopefully do. I've worried about this idea of the South in my writing since we saw each other. I have to tell you, say what I'm feeling and please know I write openly because I do love you.

Look forward to seeing you in July. If you want to talk or feel like writing, I'm here.

Much love,
Adele

Chapter 66

The deadline for the *Norton Flash Fiction Anthology* was in three days, but Tom wasn't sure he wanted to submit. Adele had sent her work already and he thought of the last journal they both submitted to. His piece was accepted and Adele's wasn't. She kissed him and said his was a fine flash and he found her later on their bed crying. "I'm sorry for being such a baby because I really am proud of you but why didn't they want mine too?" Tom was beginning to think that submission to the same place wasn't worth her depression if rejected. Their relationship quaked at these points and now the Norton call. She kept urging him to enter and said she had to learn to live with rejection in the face of his success and Tom repeated his litany. How selection is taste and pointed out the number of journals where she was published and he was turned down. Not ever to avail.

He had played competitive tennis as a kid and frequently lost so losing was a part of his history and he would go back on the court again and again. Sometimes he won. But she never played competitive anything except Scrabble. Usually beating her friends. He kept rolling over this idea of whether he should send to Norton and hoped they both would be accepted and if only one, she would be it.

Screw it. He clicked through his list of flashes, picked three, and hit send.

Chapter 67

Adele was on the floor, her back against the couch, holding the letter to Ana when Tom came in from tennis.

"What's wrong?" Tom asked.

"I can't mail this to Ana. She talked to me almost every day when I was going through chemo. She showed me the Bodhi Way."

"But that was then. This is now," Tom said, dropping to the floor across from Adele.

"I adore her."

Tom started to speak.

Adele began to tear up the letter in a methodical manner. Ripped it in half, then fourths, then eighths, as Tom did with every rejection, until her letter was shredded in a heap in front of her crossed legs. Adele entered the space where something was nothing and nothing was the essence. Where she was un-tethered. Her face paler than usual, her skin like transparent tissue. Her eyes still wet from tears wiped away before Tom got home.

"Writing the letter was enough," Adele said. "No need to mail it." She pushed the pieces closer together. "Ana was being honest. The South is what I know. It's in my bones."

Tom gathered the pieces of the letter, stood, and carried them to the trash. Adele watched him walk away in his shorts. His shirt stained with sweat.

Adele knew that time would ease the tension between Ana and her. They were like Sally and Clarissa. Always soul mates. Always there for each other. A few words that rippled the waters would vanish.

The rippling ring radiates from the center and gradually returns to quietude.

Chapter 68

Adele still wanted a child or thought she did when she saw a mother and daughter sharing a quiche at a bistro, forks poised. Their words muffled and their lips full. She watched them lean closer, turning their heads slightly to hear what the other said, and she could feel their love or thought she could as if they were wearing it just under their skin. Tom broke the silence.

"What about salmon for dinner? he asked. "I can grill it."

"What about a daughter?" she answered and watched him lick his finger, capturing flakes from his croissant.

"Daughters come from babies come from eggs, fertilized," he said

"I am fifty and have old eggs," she said and turned her head. "But look at them."

Tom's fingers caressed her shoulder, traveled down her arm, resting on her hand. He sipped his Americano remembering the 90s when he switched from briefs to boxers and placed the pillow under her, tilting Adele after sex. Side by side they would lie thirty minutes longer, giving the sperm time to catch the egg, naming rock bands from A to Z as they did on drives to the Gulf.

"We tried," he said.

She heard the relief in his voice.

Chapter 69

Tom had played doubles on his high school team but lately felt his game falling apart, torquing his knee or pulling a hamstring whenever on the court, and he'd return to the acupuncturist until the muscles were strong enough to carry him back and he'd grip the racket as if thirty years younger, no fat, no torn ligaments, a kid in white shorts smoking a Marlboro, waiting for his partner. Nearly a perfect match, Mike was tall and deliberate, game consistent from the back line while Tom, fast and aggressive, lunged for shots and covered the net. He liked, or said he liked, hitting balls with Adele. She didn't play a game, never had, too combative, and told the story of an ex who fell on his face showing her how to swing the racket for a strong serve. All she cared about was hitting the ball, hearing the occasional zing from the sweet spot.

"Your eye-hand coordination is excellent," Tom said, stuffing a few balls in his pocket. "Wish you'd run more," he said, letting the last words drop as if they were unimportant, maybe an afterthought, not really of interest. Yet she heard his discontent, his desire for a partner who'd scramble for balls, learn what competition meant, how the behavior was natural, losing part of winning. But Adele simply wanted to play, volley across the net, watch spheres move through space, slice the air at their own speed and land somewhere near, close enough that she could turn slightly, stretch her arm and strike the ball back, hoping for a distance just beyond Tom's reach.

Chapter 70

Tom clicked on an email from Esalen and found a writing weekend. Hot tubs over the Pacific, warm mineral water, skin curling under the salts, nights reading, no television, not even his cell, he and Adele without Gray between. Redwoods, ragged beach, and time.

"Want to escape to Esalen? Write all weekend?" Tom asked, looking at Adele's head lowered in Facebook, lost among 4100 friends, half the size of her hometown.

"Esalen with its brown food and public tubs," Adele said, lifting her computer off her lap, threading her fingers, her wrists lying on her stomach. Tom knew her sign of hesitation, her hands the locked gate behind which she deliberated, probably thinking of their last and only weekend there.

"The workshop's Deep Writing," he said, turning his computer to show her the description: *The group creates a genuinely safe environment because participants' writing is neither shared nor critiqued.*

Rather, the group receives permission to spend time connecting with and falling back in love with their own writing.

Adele nodded, unfolded her hands and replayed their last workshop together, not missing a frame, hearing every word Tom wrote, every word the leader spoke as an example of the best. And Adele was pulled back into a tunnel of white noise, Tom's language uttered over and over while hers was ignored, a fragment of letters stranded on a page mixed among others. Three intense days, strangers turned friends, truths explored, and the final Sunday when the leader announced he would read a couple of the appealing pieces. He read Tom's.

"I can't stand the food," Adele said. "But I'll go if you want to. Are there any other workshops?"

Chapter 71

She woke at 3 a.m. and moved her foot across the bed to encounter nothing but cold sheets. She sat up, disturbing Gray who stretched and adjusted his posture before lying down again. A faint light came into their bedroom from under Tom's study door. He was writing. She closed her eyes and lay back on the pillow, trying to envision a lake, windless at dusk. He coughed. She slipped deeper under the covers, her hand finding the cat. All Adele desired was sleep, at least five more hours—free from clutter, his writing, her writing.

How to explain this longing to be removed.

Made in the USA
Las Vegas, NV
11 October 2021